CASTLE
DIARY

*For Joan Clayton, who despite her best efforts
failed to turn her son into a pageboy*
R. P.
For William
C. R.

Text copyright © 1999 by Richard Platt
Illustrations copyright © 1999 by Chris Riddell

First U.S. small paperback edition 2003

The Library of Congress has cataloged the hardcover edition as follows:

Platt, Richard
Castle diary : the journal of Tobias Burgess, page /
transcribed by Richard Platt ; illuminated by Chris Riddell.
p.   cm.
Includes index.
Summary: As a page in his uncle's castle in thirteenth-century England, eleven-year-old
Tobias records in his journal his experiences learning how to hunt, play games of skill,
and behave in noble society. Includes notes on noblemen, castles, and feudalism.
ISBN 978-0-7636-0489-9 (hardcover)
[1. Castles — Fiction. 2. Middle Ages — Fiction.
3. Diaries — Fiction.] I. Riddell, Chris, ill. II. Title.
PZ7.P71295Cas 1999
[Fic] — dc21   98-042779
ISBN 978-0-7636-1584-0 (paperback)
ISBN 978-0-7636-2164-3 (small paperback)

13 14 15 16 17 RRH 15 14 13 12 11 10

Printed in Harrisonburg, VA, U.S.A.

This book was typeset in Truesdell, Marigold, and Francesca.
The illustrations were done in ink and watercolor.

Candlewick Press
99 Dover Street
Somerville, Massachusetts 02144

visit us at www.candlewick.com

CASTLE DIARY

The Journal of
Tobias Burgess, Page

RICHARD PLATT

illuminated by CHRIS RIDDELL

CANDLEWICK PRESS

Strandborough Castle

This Journal, being the diary of myself, Tobias Burgess, begins this day, the 2nd of January, in the year of Our Lord, 1285.

I write these words at my home in the parish of Saltington. Here I dwell with my father Henry, my mother Gwynedd, and my two younger sisters, Edythe and Sian.

But soon I shall be leaving here, for I am to spend the next twelvemonth (and more, I hope) as a page at the castle of my father's elder brother, John Burgess, Baron of Strandborough.

My uncle has expected me these past two years, but my mother wept and would not let me go. In just two days, though, I shall be eleven years of age, and my father says I can wait no longer. At last I am to be taught the skills and duties I must know to become a squire and even, mayhap, a knight — if my father can afford it!

My mother bids me write this journal so that I will remember all that passes, and can tell her of it when I see her next. For though Strandborough Castle is not twenty miles distant, 'tis most difficult country to cross and, as few people journey that way, news from there is scarce.

Now all that stops me is the weather, for the snow lies so thickly on the ground that the roads can barely be seen, let alone traveled upon! The delay tries both my patience and that of Hugh, my father's servant, whose task it is to deliver me to Strandborough. Though I shall be sad to leave my family (except for my sister Sian, who vexes me daily), I scarce can wait to begin my new life.

January 10th, Wednesday

Our arrival made me feel most grand, for when we were yet some distance away, the watchman did spy us out and sound his horn, and my cousin Simon rode out to greet us. Simon is full-grown and soon to be a knight, but I was greatly pleased to see him as he was kind to me when last he visited my father.

We entered the castle through a great gateway and into the Bailey beyond — my father's manor house, and his stables, would fit easily in this huge courtyard.

At the far end stands a strong tower house called the Keep. Within the Keep is the Great Hall, which is used for eating and other gatherings. The family live in newer dwellings built against the South Wall. Here Simon showed me where I would sleep and left me. I share my room with three other pages. We sleep on wooden pallets with mattresses of straw, like at home.

I confess I am so tired from the journey that I barely have strength to write these words.

January 11th, Thursday

I awoke this morning early and had chance to observe the other pages while they slept. The one who woke next shared some bread with me. He told me his name was Mark and asked me mine. As we ate he pointed at the other sleeping pages, and laughed: "See Toby — Oliver and Humphrey shall have no bread, for they slumber still."

Soon Simon came to take me to the Great Hall, where my Aunt Elizabeth sat by a huge fire. She welcomed me fondly and told me that my uncle attends the King in the west of the country but will return in a few days.

Then my aunt bade me greet my other cousins, Simon's sisters, Abigail and Beth. Abigail, who is the fairer of face, is younger than I, and her sister is older. When we were introduced Abigail blushed and looked at me from the tail of her eye. "Toby is here to learn the duties of a page," my aunt told them, "but this day I would like you to show him our home." Then, turning to me, she added that on the morrow I would learn what I must do to make myself useful.

January 12th, Friday

I find that everyone calls my uncle and aunt "My Lord" and "My Lady," and that I must do likewise. There are so many strange things to learn and do here that today I have time to write only a line or two. I fear my journal will have many gaps in it!

January 13th, Saturday

Directly after we had broken our fast yesterday, my aunt summoned me and spoke to me of my duties. Pages here serve my aunt and uncle, and thus learn courtesy and the manners and customs of a noble family.

Like the other pages, I am expected to make myself useful by running errands and carrying messages and suchlike. At mealtimes I will learn to serve my aunt and uncle and their guests — to fill their cups and carve them slices of meat which I will place before them in a genteel way.

But as I am her nephew, I am also to be my aunt's

personal page and
must hold myself
ready at all times
to attend her.
(Though I
thought this
an honour,
Humphrey — who is the
oldest of the pages here — scorned it,
saying my aunt will have a sharper eye than most for my
errors.)

Much of this seemed to me to be dull stuff, so I asked
my aunt if I might also ride in a hunt. She did not answer
but instead told me of my studies. The castle Chaplain is
away at present, for he visits with the Bishop, but on his
return I will join the other pages under his tutelage.
With this, my aunt bade me make myself familiar with
the many buildings and places within the castle walls,
and then dismissed me.

January 14th, The Lord's Day

This noon 'twas my task to serve my aunt at table, though I fear that through the nervous shaking of my hand as much food fell to the floor as was placed before her.

The Hall was crowded, for there are many servants here, and it will be some days before I will properly know one from t'other. Only two of them are women, and one is constantly at my aunt's side. This woman, whose name is Isbel, dresses finely in clothes quite like my aunt's. The other is Isbel's maid. She wears clothes of red and blue, the same colors as the uniforms of many of the men servants.

I found it very odd that my aunt's servant should herself have a servant. But when I asked my aunt to explain she answered me sharply, saying, "Watch your tongue! Though she does my bidding, Isbel is no peasant girl. She is as much my companion as my servant. Like you and many others who serve your uncle and me, she comes from a good family and is used to soft clothes and being waited upon." Then my aunt said, "Why, even a servant's servants sometimes need servants!"

And 'twas true, as I soon discovered. The Steward, for instance, who seems a prim and fussy man, is the most senior of the servants and is in charge of I know not how many others. Among those he

instructs is the Butler, whose duty it is to care for the castle wines and ales. The Butler in turn commands the Cellarer, who stores the wine. And even the Cellarer has boys to lift the barrels for him.

All but the lowest servants eat together in the Hall, and we pages sit with them when our serving duties are done.

January 15th, Monday

I attended my aunt today in the Great Chamber. This is
where my aunt and uncle sleep, but by day my aunt
receives visitors there and instructs the servants in the
running of the castle. At home we call this room the
Solar, though ours is smaller by far. My aunt is always
busy, for it is she who directs the Steward in the
management of the castle household. She jokes that
when my uncle is away she must do all her own work
and also everything he does — except for shaving!

January 16th, Tuesday

With my aunt again this day and met more of the people
who aid her in her daily busy-ness. Within the walls, it is
the Constable who minds the castle when my aunt and
uncle are both away at their other estates. When my
aunt told him who I was, he did not smile or speak, but
sighed deeply as if I had already wronged him.

With him also was the Reeve. This man has charge of

all the manor — the farms and forest and common lands belonging to the castle. The Reeve collects the rents and taxes which those who dwell on the manor must pay to my uncle regularly for their housing and farms — and for other privileges such as the right to collect firewood in the forest.

January 17th, Wednesday

Today returned my uncle. When I was summoned to greet him, he clapped me firmly on the shoulder and told me that I would make a fine page.

I asked him if I could have a horse (much missing my own pony, which Hugh had taken home) and when I could ride in a hunt. But he laughed and said only: "Patience lad, thou shalt learn of such things in time."

My uncle says I am to study archery and mayhap fighting with a sword, for I shall need these noble skills when I become a squire and learn the craft of knight-hood. Knights serve the King and do battle against his foes. But they must be honorable as well as brave, so squires also study the rules of chivalry — which means doing noble deeds and helping and respecting everyone.

January 20th, Saturday

This day returned the Chaplain to lead our daily worship. He it is who has the task of teaching us pages, as well as writing letters for my aunt when she is busy with her other duties. Now not only must we rise an hour earlier each morn to attend Mass, but schooling will begin again soon!

January 22nd, Monday

This day I spent in schooling with the other pages and with my cousins Abigail and Beth. If we have no other duties, we start our studies after Mass and breaking fast, and continue as long as there is daylight enough to read by.

Chaplain teaches us Latin and the Scriptures. We also study our letters with him, and our numbers. My mother has taught me well in reading and writing in English and

I am ahead of most (excepting Beth, who is most studious for a girl), but Latin is new to me, and I must learn many pages of the most dull books.

January 23rd, Tuesday

Studying today was no better than yesterday. It seems that most of my days will be taken up like this until my fourteenth birthday. Then I shall become a squire (if I do not die from boredom first). Mark whispered to me that all schooling, everywhere, is like this. The Chaplain, seeing us speak, did thrash me, but I did not cry out. Later Mark warned me that Chaplain beats us more in winter. "'Tis surely because the room is cold, and whipping warms both his arms and our rumps," said Mark!

January 24th, Wednesday

This forenoon a squire fetched me during our Latin studies. He said that my uncle has commanded a HUNT for Saturday, and I should make haste to the stables to try out the horse they had for me!

My heart leaped at this. At home, Mother forbids me to ride with hounds (even though Father would allow it), for she fears I shall fall.

The stables lie along the North Wall and are grander and in better repair than many cottages I have seen. Here they keep many different kinds of horses, for sport and for work. The horses, too, look less hungry than the people who labour in the fields, and are certainly cleaner.

The man who has charge of the stables is called the "Sergeant-Farrier," and such is his skill, Mark tells me, that many outside the castle seek his advice when their horses fall sick.

The greatest of the horses are two huge warhorses, called destriers, that my uncle rides in battle. There are also three lesser horses, called palfreys, that he uses when he is not riding in the King's service. Then there are coursers for hunting, gentle hackneys for ladies to ride, and great numbers of packhorses and carthorses.

Sergeant-Farrier brought me Prancer, who is a courser. She is a fine horse, bigger and much better bred than my nag, Hobby, at home. He led me out into the Bailey. Then, seeing I could handle her, he let me ride out through the gatehouse and across the meadows beyond.

Prancer is much faster than Hobby, too, and in my excitement I did not notice that my hat had taken flight from my head. When I had retrieved it, I galloped on across the fields and tried to imagine myself leading the chase!

January 25th, Thursday

Humphrey and Oliver made great sport last night about my horse and the hunt. They pretend they have no wish to "tear their clothes and muddy themselves in the

destrier

courser

hackney

palfrey

packhorse

forest." But they make fun of me because in truth they too wish to hunt, and I am promised this adventure only because I am my uncle's nephew.

January 26th, Friday

Was teased without mercy again today, but this time by Mark because (he says) while sleeping I did gallop as if my bed were a horse, and woke them all by shouting "HOO STO!" and other such hunting calls.

For lateness at school Mark was punished with the finger pillory. I laughed, and for this had to join him. Chaplain made us stand one hour with our fingers held tight between the pillory's boards.

I fear I shall sleep as little as a cat this night. For my mind spins with thoughts of the morrow's venture. I pray that it will be a success.

January 27th, Saturday

The baying of hounds woke me before dawn this day, and I opened the shutter just in time to see the kennel-lads fixing bells around the dogs' necks, which I thought most odd.

Breakfast was a much grander affair than the bread and ale that we usually enjoy, for gathered with my uncle in the Hall were many other noble folk from neighboring manors.

The talk was all of THE HUNT. It seems that my uncle's manor is a better place than most for such sport. He and his squires hunt deer or hare or fox each week at least, though rarely with so many noble friends. Today, though, we were to hunt BOAR, which is the most exciting and dangerous of all quarry. (This, I learned, is why the dogs wear bells — the noise of them scares the

beast, which otherwise is so fierce it will kill half the pack!)

At last the signal was given and the hunt set off. We rode from the castle to the forest's edge before releasing the hounds. But then, though I followed as fast as I dared, I was soon left far behind.

Ahead of me I could hear the hounds baying with great excitement, and I guessed they had found a boar. Then I heard the Huntsman signal the end of the chase with a long note on his horn, and I knew I had missed the best moment.

The tracks of the
horses led me to a clearing
where the Huntsman had already cut
open the beast and given its guts to the
dogs. A squire I did not know told me the boar
had fought bravely, turning at the end to face the
pack. But the hounds had kept the boar at bay until the
huntsmen could surround it and kill it with spears and
swords. I was sore dismayed not to have seen such a sight.

What's more, I lost my way on the journey back to the
castle. 'Twas dusk before I returned, and now I have had no
supper!

February 5th, Monday

Chaplain sickened this forenoon and took to his bed, so we were free to do as we pleased. To help me forget my misery over the hunt (and because he was sick of hearing me tell of it), Mark offered to teach me longshanks — this being his name for stilts.

He led me to the old sally port in the West Wall. This small door was once a back way out of the castle but is scarce used today.

We went to the little wood that grows beyond the wall and there Mark showed me how to cut a forked chestnut branch, with one side long to hold on to, and the other short to stand on. I soon discovered that my stilts were far more easily made than used, though, and have bruises aplenty to show for it!

February 6th, Tuesday

Back to schooling this day. Sitting in the cold Keep fair
freezed me to the bone, so when lessons were ended I
slipped into the kitchen. While thawing in its warmth I
watched a kitchen-lad making pie shells, which he did call
coffins.

Not many minutes had passed before the Cook espied
me heating myself by the bread oven. He asked my
business there and when he learned that I had no task
said, "There is no room in my kitchen for useless
bodies," and set me to copying from a pile of recipes that
he had. They were much splattered and a few even
smelled of the dishes they described. Some were most
strange, especially a salad made with cocks' combs and
hens' feet.

For writing on, Cook gave me some old scraps of
parchment. Many had to be scraped clean before I could
use them again.

February 13th, Tuesday

Before lessons I went again to warm myself in the kitchen and watched while Cook made bread. He and his helpers start work before dawn, and the kitchen was a busy, bustling place. Cook mixes water and flour with barm. This last stuff he gets from the Brewess in the village, who calls it yeast. Her work is to make ale for the castle, and as it brews she scoops off the barm that floats on the top as foam. This barm forms bubbles that swell the dough, making the bread light. Cook kneads the dough in a trough made of the hollowed-out half of a tree-trunk, then shapes it into loaves and leaves it to rise.

February 14th, Wednesday

Cook showed me today how they bake bread. A kitchen-lad lights the oven early on baking days, so that it is hot when the loaves are ready for baking.

He begins by burning bundles of sticks and then throws in a log or two. As soon as the oven glows over

all, he scoops out the embers, brushes out most of the gray ash, then wipes the oven floor with a wet mop. The oven hisses mightily, and steam issues from its mouth like the breath of a dragon. Cook then sets the loaves into the hot oven with a wooden shovel he calls a peel.

They bake here three kinds of bread. Cook made me miniature loaves of each sort, and all the kitchen staff rested at their work to watch me taste them. The best, called manchet, is made from sifted wheaten flour and is the white bread we eat in Hall. The second, brown cheat bread, I knew also, for I have seen some of the servants eat it.

The last, which I did not
know, they call brom-bread. It
was horrible and I spat it out,
which caused great mirth
among those who watched.

I learned later that only dogs and horses eat such
bread. It is baked to use up the bran the miller sieves out
from the wheat when he makes white flour. At such ill-use
I ran out of the kitchen and vowed not to go back there
even if the ice freezes off all my fingers!

February 21st, Wednesday

Tomorrow I am to spend the day at the butts (which is
what they call the archery targets here), and must do so in
the company of the Constable. Part of his work as warden
of the castle is to train the castle guards and ensure that
they are constantly ready to ward off an attack. To this
end, he and his men practice their fighting skills as often
as the weather and their other duties will allow.

To him also is given the task of instructing us pages in the basic points of archery, though clearly he does not relish such a chore, for when my uncle asked him to watch over me at the butts, he protested loudly. He said that I was old enough to look after myself (which is true).

But my uncle silenced him, saying, "Hush, man, 'tis just for one day! Once he has the hang of it he can practice without your help. But this is my brother's only son. What say he if the lad be spiked with an arrow on his first day at yonder butts?"

February 22nd, Thursday

This morn the Constable and I ventured out together to the butts beyond the North Wall (each of us pretending that we were alone).

At home I have a bow which Father fashioned for me, but when I saw what they call here a "boy's bow," I knew mine was but a toy.

My new bow is made of yew wood, and is as tall as me. Straight as an iron rod, it is almost as stiff. To bend it and fit the string takes all my strength.

My arrows are the perfect twins of those the castle guards use, but done in miniature. They have real goose-feather flights, which are supposed to make them fly straight at the target.

Oftener, though, my arrows fly elsewhere when I let go the bow string. I had thought that my practice with arrows in the orchard at home last summer might be some help to me in this new endeavour, but I am by far the poorest archer in the castle!

March 3rd, Saturday

Have been neglectful of my journal of late, for studies and other tasks fill the daylight hours when it is light enough to write. I made this entry in school while I did pretend to be studying my numbers.

At the butts yesterday one of the archers showed me why his kind are so feared by our King's foes. With bow in hand he stood before a tree with a trunk thicker than my chest. He pulled back the bow string until the veins stood out upon his face, and when he loosed the arrow, its head passed clean through the tree-trunk and pierced the other side.

Seeing this, the other archers jeered that he was showing off, and four more of them repeated his trick. But then when he let fly thirteen arrows in a minute none took up his challenge to better him.

March 9th, Friday

Practiced archery again today. This time I was much

better and pulled the string right back. But when the Constable saw this he gave me a bigger bow, so once again I am the castle dizzard at the butts.

Of twelve arrows I shot with my new bow, only four hit target, while seven fell on grass. One killed a sparrow in flight. Those watching cried "HAIL!" and clapped, so I bowed low to them and said not that 'twas but a fluke.

March 11th, The Lord's Day

With much ceremony a special dish was placed before me at dinner today. Baked on a skewer was the bird that I had shot. Cook, whose jest this was, called it "Sparrow à l'Arrow." And though there was scarce a mouthful of meat on the bird, it tasted well.

March 12th, Monday

This morn I overheard my uncle say he was to visit the
castle armory to see about some small changes to his
helm. He wishes it to weigh less heavy on his head, yet
better protect him at the JOUSTS!

Of this tournament I knew nothing and I begged his
leave to accompany him. In my excitement I quite forgot
myself and began to say, "Uncle, tell me more about…,"
for I desired most keenly to learn of these jousts. But
then I remembered my manners, and blushing, began
anew: "My Lord, if it pleases you, pray tell me more
about the tournament."

This made him laugh, and he spoke freely about it,
saying that the jousts are to be held, as usual, on Saint
George's feast day. So I must wait SIX WEEKS!

Within the armory they make and mend all manner of
weapons as well as armor. But the noise of hammering
and the heat from the furnace in which they soften the
metal were so great that they made my head whirl. 'Tis

certain the sound has made the Armorer and the Smith and their apprentices as deaf as beetles, for to make himself heard my uncle had to bellow like a braying ass.

March 16th, Friday

My cousin Beth hath sewed me a shirt of Egyptiacal cotton! I have never before had such dainty garb. I hastened to put it on, but because it is new the seams and stitches rubbed my skin sore.

Humphrey and Oliver both laughed at this and called me "chrisomer" and "nigget" and "moonling." They are accustomed to new clothes and will suffer them until washing softens the folds. But I would rather wear my old linen shirt, for though it is more common, 'tis also more comfortable.

March 19th, Monday

Played at knights with Mark, Oliver, and Humphrey today. As Mark is bigger than me, he was the horse and I rode his back. We won. Oliver toppled from his horse and got a bloody nose. Serves him right, for he did twist my ears most painfully and call me the worst names when first I wore my new shirt.

March 20th, Tuesday

Wrote yesternight by candle's flicker and fell asleep with quill in hand. When I awoke, the candle had set the pages alight, and would have burned my straw mattress or worse if Humphrey had not smelled smoke and beat out the flames. This morning Chaplain likewise beat my backside — to teach me care with candles, he said.

Ate salt fish again today. DISGUSTING! Here they are more careful to follow the Church's rules than at home, so besides every Tuesday, Friday, and Saturday being fish days, they also eat fish on each Church festival. This means we eat vile fish more often than flesh or fowl.

April 11th, Wednesday

Watched my uncle practice for the jousts today. He
charged eleven times at a wooden ring hung from a tree
and caught it on his lance five times. It takes much skill
to lift the ring from it's hook while galloping at full speed,
and all who saw this agree it bodes well for the contest.

April 22nd, The Lord's Day

Tomorrow begin the jousts! The host of noble knights
who accepted my uncle's challenge are lodged at inns
nearby or are encamped upon the fields outside the castle.

TWO-SCORE gaily coloured tents sprouted in the night like mushrooms. Flying from lances planted in the ground, the knights' pennants look like flowers in a spring meadow.

All the talk is of who shall prevail, and methinks the men of the castle guard place wagers on the winner. I pray my uncle shall vanquish them all!

April 23rd, Monday

This being the feast day of Saint George, the whole castle was astir well before sunrise in preparation for the jousts.

All the clashes were keenly fought, but I shall give account of my uncle's combat first. His opponent was Lord Sudbury. Everyone from the castle (and the village folk besides) gathered eagerly to watch their charge.

After some ceremony, of which I shall tell later, the two knights trotted to opposite ends of the Lists (which is what they call the strip of field where the combat takes place). When they were some 300 paces apart, they turned to face each other.

The sunlight danced on their shiny helms, and on the bright colors of their families' arms blazoned on their shields and armor.

On the command "LAISSEZ ALLER" from a herald, both knights urged their horses forward. Pricked with sharp spurs, the snorting horses galloped faster and faster until they ran as swift as a March gale. Each knight aimed his lance at the shield of the other, and the watchers cried "HUZZAH!" when my uncle stayed on his horse and knocked Sudbury to the ground. Three times my uncle toppled Sudbury.

At their third meeting, though, the force of Sudbury's blow lifted my uncle, too, clean from his saddle.

Those who watched gasped "ALAS!" in fear for my uncle's life, but he quickly rose to his feet and raised his iron glove to still the hubbub.

Then, though, he found that he could not raise the visor on his helm, so twisted it was from the fall. And when later the heralds announced that my uncle was the victor, he was nowhere to be found.

At length, a search of the castle discovered my uncle in the armory — with his head laid on an anvil and the Smith at work upon his helm. 'Tis surely a wonder the Smith could remove it without harming a hair on my uncle's head.

April 25th, Wednesday

There seems each day of the jousts to be less sport than the day before, and more boring ceremony. Before combat begins each morn, the knights withdraw to their arming tents, where a squire helps him dress for the jousts. When they return, fully armed, there is much bowing low and making of speeches. When these dull preparations are complete, the heralds proclaim the names of the combatants, whose faces are hidden behind their shiny helms.

Only then do the first two knights face each other and spur their horses on, and to my mind the excitement that follows is over far too soon.

April 26th, Thursday

The jousting ends at last! I swear I should die of boredom if I were to listen to just one more speech. And after so many charges all knights look the same. If I had known it would be thus, I should have feigned illness on Monday and so escaped the ordeal.

The new hose that I wear for this grand event is hot, for it clings to my legs as tightly as the skin clings to a sausage. And it is my duty to wait upon my aunt all day while she watches, which tires me much.

Gilbert, Earl of Hertford, was this day mortally wounded in the jousts. But when I talked of it with Mark he only said: "Well, 'tis common."

May 3rd, Thursday

Today was an Egypty day. And as all know, ill fortune follows any work that starts on these two unlucky days in the month. Our Chaplain cautioned us that 'twas but a superstition from heathen Egypt. My uncle also told us we should not mind it. Later, though, I heard him tell a groom to put away the horses he had saddled, for only fools start journeys on Egypty days.

May 14th, Monday

While we studied this forenoon my cousin Abigail

scratched a message in her wax tablet and passed it to me. Chaplain seized it and now I must rise before dawn for a week and pray with him. This seems to me most UNJUST! I am punished, though I did no wrong. She did wrong, yet is not punished.

May 27th, The Lord's Day

Yesterday was one of great celebration, for my uncle dubbed Simon a knight. Now he is twenty-one, Simon has been full seven years a squire and has learned well the noble skills of knighthood.

Two days did Simon spend in prayer and fasting. On Friday night he slept not at all, but kept vigil in the Chapel, praying until dawn. Then, at cock-crow, he bathed and dressed in a tunic of pure white, and attended Mass. Only after this could he break his fast and venture out into the Bailey for the armoring ceremony.

First, my uncle dressed him in a coat of mail. Then Simon put on a gleaming helm and gilded spurs, and

grasped a shield painted with the two Burgess ravens.
When this was done he knelt to await the colee — the
blow from my uncle's sword that would make him a
knight.

I thought this would be no more than a light tap and
was alarmed to see how heavy was the blow. But Simon
was expecting it thus. He rose speedily, and swore a
solemn vow to be a gallant and brave knight. Then all
cheered as he mounted a fine Spanish palfrey and rode
round the Bailey. Later, there was feasting in the Hall in

Simon's honor. He will make a fine knight; and he is a good and kind cousin.

June 9th, Saturday

The weather of late has been fearsome hot. We have not seen a cloud in weeks, and the ground is parched from want of rain. The river has sunk lower than any can remember, and green SLIME grows in that part of the moat where we usually swim.

In the Bailey two men dig a new well. This is oft a wet and muddy task, but as there is little water to fill the well the men can work dry-foot.

June 13th, Wednesday

The garderobes all reek. When I have need of them I rush in nimbly, clutching my nose. I let fall my hose and pray that relief will be quick. This forenoon when I sat upon the wooden seat, out from under it flew a black fly so fat that at first I took it to be a wren.

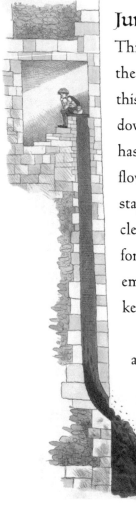

June 15th, Friday

This day the GONG-FARMER came from
the village to work below the South Wall. On
this side of the castle the garderobes empty
down chutes into the moat. But because there
has been no rain, the moat is sluggish in its
flow and everything that falls from the chutes
stays where it drops. The Gong-Farmer must
clear not only these piles but others besides,
for elsewhere in the castle the garderobes
empty into pits, which must be cleaned to
keep them sweet.

One of the garderobe chutes is blocked
and the Gong-Farmer must reach up inside
this slimy pipe to unclog it. I would not
do his job for all the King's gold.
A humming black cloud hangs
always above a Gong-
Farmer's head. Nose

warns of his approach long before eyes espy him, and all ears are alert to the squeaking of his stinking cart.

June 20th, Wednesday
Woke two nights past to the crashing of thunder. Now the rain does not stop and we are awash with water!

July 9th, Monday
Today at table my aunt and uncle talked softly mouth to ear. Isbel, my aunt's companion, has told me that a grand Earl is coming to Strandborough. He and his household are journeying north and will rest at the castle for at least two nights. I divined from their talk that my aunt and uncle are already planning a great banquet for the visit, even though 'tis still some weeks away.

July 14th, Saturday
This morn my aunt told Isbel the reason for my uncle's keen preparations, and as she is friendly towards me Isbel

has entrusted me also with the secret. It seems this great Earl has the ear of the King, and my uncle hopes to gain favor by welcoming him. Though my uncle's castle is grand, this Earl has an estate many times larger. As there are pebbles on a beach, so he has gold coins in equal numbers.

July 20th, Friday

Isbel tutored me in table manners this day (though I needed it not). "If you eat with the Earl's household while they are here," said she, "have a care to spit politely on the floor, not over the table."

When I sniffed, she reminded me that if I should wipe my nose, it is only seemly to clean my hand on my clothes before touching food.

July 27th, Friday

Towards the end of lessons today we heard music from beyond the castle walls. Abigail and I made haste to find out whence had come this sound, and Simon told us that

a band of players had passed by on their way to the
village inn. They have come at my uncle's bidding for the
banquet. These folk journey near and far, singing for
their bread, and Simon has said he will take us to see
them on the morrow.

July 28th, Saturday

We found the players outside the village church, amusing a
crowd of folk. The tumblers were most marvelous and
though one showed me how he walks on his hands, I could
not master even one step.

The minstrels sang of our King's victory in the west.
Their verses brought news, too, of wars and great
happenings in other lands. Most songs were jolly, though,
and the crowd that was gathered there knew them of old
and joined in with the choruses.

A few folk dropped a farthing in a leathern hat which the
tumblers passed around. Others gave them bread or cheese,
or brought a jug of ale to pay for this fine entertainment.

July 30th, Monday

Today, two great ox-carts trundled across the drawbridge to the kitchen yard. It took Cook's servants near half the day to unload and store all the provisions for the feast. The first cart bore barrels of wine and ale so large they had to be rolled for they could not be lifted. The second cart held all manner of meats and fish. One was most strange, with the tail of a fish but the fur of a beast and the face of a man with whiskers complete. Later, Cook told me 'twas some kind of sea beast. 'Tis fantastical food we shall be eating when at last we sit down at our trenchers!

On Wednesday arrives the Earl, and on Thursday will be the banquet.

August 7th, Tuesday

These five days past the whole household supped in Hall in honor of our most noble guest, the Earl of Branstone.

But straightway after the feast a fever afflicted me and I was taken to lie in the Great Chamber, where my aunt and Isbel could watch over me. Though somewhat recovered, I am as weak as a kitten and must stay in bed — so shall use the time to write of past events, for I fear I neglect my journal. The feast itself was the grandest thing I have ever seen. I could not help but stare at the many fine clothes and the gold and silver dishes.

It was the food, though, that caused all present to gasp in amazement and marvel at the seemingly endless array of dishes. Here were majestic peacocks, stuffed and roasted and proudly dressed in their feathers, and there the tiny tongues of larks. And fish of all kinds in plenty, baked and boiled, and platter after platter of roasted meats rich with sauces.

The Earl had come with a host of servants who helped us bring out the dishes for each course. Each dish was carried in with much ceremony and presented to my uncle and the Earl before it was served. When the dishes were laid on the tables we sat down to eat.

There were a great many dishes I did not recognize. One seemed half bird, half beast. Mark named it: "Cockatrice 'tis called, but I know not where it is hunted." This made Humphrey laugh so hard that he almost spat out his food. "Mark!" he snorted. "'Tis but a kitchen trick. First they pluck a big fowl and cut it across the waist. Then they take a piglet, likewise cut in half, and sew top of one to bottom of t'other."

This cockatrice tasted good, but the noble Earl would not eat of it (or of any other dish) before his butler had tasted it to see if it was fit for his master.

I tire now and so shall write more upon the morrow.

August 8th, Wednesday

I have told how grandly we ate at the feast. But in a few ways this banquet was like ordinary fare. As usual, of course, we ate with knife, spoon, and fingers and heaped our food upon trenchers of hard, stale cheat bread cut into thick slices.

Drink, too, was much the same. But instead of the weak penny ale that is all we pages are normally allowed, the cup-bearers poured us twopenny ale, which tasted far stronger.

As it grew later the ale loosened everyone's tongues, and Humphrey and Oliver began to make rude fun of me. When I sat with my legs apart, Oliver did point to where they joined beneath my thin hose. With much glee he chanted: "Let not thy privy members be laid open to be viewed. 'Tis most shameful and abhorred, detestable and rude!"

The tail of this rhyme I scarcely heard, for just then the minstrels blew a fanfare. Both they and the tumblers had been entertaining us all most skilfully (though some of the minstrels' songs were saucy and made the ladies blush and bashfully study the floor).

The horns that drowned Oliver's words announced a subtlety. The subtleties were cunningly fashioned from sugar and almond paste and were one of the delicacies that ended each of the four courses.

They were goodly sweet to taste, though they did not look like food at all. One was modeled as a hunting scene, and another as a mythic beast. But my favorite was one that looked like a great ship tossed at sea.

After the fanfare I remember no more, for this was when (or so I am told) I sickened and fell headlong to the floor.

August 9th, Thursday

Because I am still weak and do not mend as quickly as
my aunt would wish, my uncle has sent Simon to fetch a
physician from Middlethorpe.

This town is but an hour's ride from Strandborough,
though my uncle said that as he doubts I am dying,
Simon need not rush to return before tomorrow.

August 10th, Friday

The Physician arrived today. Leach he is called and the
name describes him well, for he is round and sleek and I
like him not!

First he had me relieve myself into a glass flask so he
could study my water. He held it up to the window to
judge the color, and then brought it to his nose. I
guessed he would drink from it next, but instead he set it
down on the table. Then he took from his purse a folded
piece of parchment and, opening it, studied its
mysterious signs and marks with great care.

He asked when the sickness began, and for the day, hour, and place of my birth. From another chart he worked out how stood the stars when I sickened (for this also affects his choice of cure). Then he announced: "The boy is melancholic, and Earth fights Fire for control of his body." This surprised me not a little, for I had thought it was the surfeit of food and ale I had swallowed at the banquet that ailed my gut.

Finally he added that I should be bled, but as this was not a favorable time for such a task he would return, if needed, in a few days.

August 12th, The Lord's Day
Still I am confined to my bed in the Great Chamber. When I tried to rise this morn, the room swung so

wildly about me that I felt sick to my stomach again and my aunt straightway made me lie back down.

Today my aunt received a visitor. This woman, who is called Lady Cecily, is my aunt's friend and lives in the neighboring manor of Littlethorpe. She brought with her a younger sister, Jane. Together the four women wiled away the day in working at their needlepoint and playing chess and backgammon. Mostly, though, they gossiped of the banquet and of the noble knights they knew. Later, Jane and Isbel tried to teach me backgammon, but my brain was too muddled to make much sense of it.

When they went to eat in the Hall, Mark sneaked in to see how I did, which cheered me greatly.

August 13th, Monday

Doctor Leach came again today, and after much peering and prodding, he declared once more that I must be bled to release the ill humors or fluids that are in my body. Grasping hold of my arm, he straightway chose a vein and opened it with a knife. He told my aunt that this would let out the black bile, of which I have too much. And that as the moon is nearly full, this is a good time for bloodletting.

At length the Leach bandaged up my arm and, taking out a piece of parchment, wrote the letters of my name on it. Then he gave each of the letters a number, summed them all together, and announced: "The boy shall live!"

At this my aunt near swooned with joy, and paid the fat Doctor well for his work. But I feel sicker than ever and my arm hurts abominably.

August 16th, Thursday

Today I am much mended, though my arm still pains me not a little. I cannot think how bleeding someone helps to cure them. 'Tis my belief I am recovered in spite of Doctor Leach's treatment rather than because of it.

August 24th, Friday

Though I am now full recovered, I did this morn feign illness. The day was bright and clear, and after so much time indoors I had no heart for spending more in dull schooling.

While my cousins and the other pages were at their studies, I slipped out and walked along the river bank toward the forest.

The wheat stands high and yellow in the fields, for reaping will soon begin. At first I saw no one, and had only the skylarks and rabbits for company. But then I spied some sudden movement in the distance and, being curious, made haste to find out what it was.

When I drew closer I spied a man lying on the river bank. He was now perfectly still, gazing into the water. His hand was in the water, too, and near it a fish stirred.

The fish swam right up to the man and over his hand. Suddenly the silence ended, and all was splashing as the man hurled the flapping fish on to the bank.

The poacher (for such I guessed he was) sprang to his feet and then saw me. He looked at me and I at him. We two looked at the fish, which thrashed on the grass. He stooped and picked up the wriggling fish and, swinging it by the tail, brought its head down on a tree-stump.

The fish went still, and he laid it down next to another one.

"Thou hast not seen me, hast thou boy?" he growled. I did not understand him and said nothing. At this he swore beneath his breath and raised his fist. "Thou hast not seen me, nor the fish!"

I turned, but before I could run his hand shot out and grabbed my arm. Then he knelt down and, bringing his face close to mine, began to talk more calmly.

"Now lad, thou shouldst not be here, shouldst thou?" he questioned.

He smelled of onions and ale, and though his voice was soft his grip was not, so I confessed it was the truth.

"Well, then," he said, "you keep us meeting here a secret and so shall I. Agreed?"

I wished he would let go my arm, so promised I'd say nothing. When his grip slackened I burst free and hurried back to the castle.

August 26th, The Lord's Day

This coming week the harvesting begins and the castle wheat will be cut. I pleaded with my aunt to let me go into the fields and help, as I do at home.

She said at first 'twas not right for a boy of my good birth to work in the fields. But seeing that I craved it she did bend and bade me tell the Reeve that I could join the castle harvest for a day when work began.

August 28th, Tuesday

I asked Oliver about fishing. He told me that all of the
fish in the river belong to the castle — not just those in
the stewponds fed by the moat's waters. Poachers steal
many fish, he said, and they go to a different place each
time so the Water-Keeper cannot catch them. He said the
poachers grill their stolen fish on a single leek leaf, which
holds it like a boat. I did not believe him, but when I
asked Mark he swore it was true.

August 29th, Wednesday

The villagers hasten to cut their own wheat, while the
Reeve mutters and peers at the skies. For when Reeve
feels the time is right, they must leave their harvesting
and reap the castle wheat instead. 'Tis called a "boon,"
which means my uncle commands the villagers to do this
work for nothing — it is their ancient duty and they
cannot refuse.

Cook and Brewess both curse, for all those who

harvest have a great thirst and hunger. By custom the castle must feed them and quench their thirst on a boon-day. But Mark says 'tis not all work, and there shall be some sport when the castle harvest is done. This is all that he will tell me, and he only smiles when I beg to know more.

September 3rd, Monday

The past four days being hot, the Reeve held off from the boon-work to let the wheat dry further before it was cut. But today he would wait no longer, and straightway after Mass I hurried to the fields.

Already many people flocked around. The Reeve shouted at them to hasten, for he wanted near twenty acres cut today. The Reeve directs the harvest, just as he does most other business between castle and village.

I saw the poacher I had met by the river. He stepped up to me and said quietly: "Come, lad. I did not mean to frighten thee t'other day." His voice was gentle, and I was

glad to know someone in such a large crowd of strangers.
Seeing us talk, Reeve called out: "Ho, David! Thou and
Toby are unlikely friends." There was much laughter at
this, but David clapped me on the back and replied: "Aye,
and he offers to bind my wheat this day." So I set to work
as a poacher's helper.

Everyone worked fast. The reapers bent double,
grasping the stalks near the ground before cutting them.
David watched me until he saw that I knew how to shake
out the weeds and use the stalks themselves to tie up
each bundle.

Folk paused from time to time to sharpen their sickles or mop their brows and drink from stone jars. For though the sky was dull the day was hot, and the work warmed them.

At noon, everyone rested and ate. Cook had set out mountains of bread, cheese, and meat on wide boards laid across barrels. All who harvested could eat their fill of castle food, and wash it down with plentiful ale. The village folk drained in one day a barrel of ale so large it stood higher than my head.

The field in which we worked is 300 long paces across and as many wide, yet no more than forty men had cut all the wheat by dusk.

When it was done, each reaper took as his right one sheaf of wheat for each half-acre he had cut. David cursed as he lifted his. "This is miser's pay for such hard work," he said. I asked him what he meant.

"Boon-work is our duty, Toby lad," he replied. "None does it willingly. Each man has his own strips of land,

and to eat we must labor hard. Just when our crop is ready to be cut, so too is the castle's. But we gain nothing from the wheat we cut today, for it feeds the castle folk." And with this he bade me goodnight.

September 4th, Tuesday

Today ended the boon-work. I slipped out to the fields as soon as lessons were over and, as Mark had said, there was a game.

As the sun was setting, the Reeve stood in the middle of the field and tossed high a sickle. With wheat sheaves we marked a ring as wide as his throw was long. Then Reeve fetched a ewe and set her in the middle of the ring.

David bade me keep still and watch what happened next. "If sheep stays in ring until cock crows, the villagers keep her," he whispered. "But if she runs, 'twill be to yonder table," and he pointed up at the castle. None dared move save the Reeve. He coughed loudly, but it did not fright the ewe.

We had not long to wait, for in any village there are plenty of cocks, and before a moment was out one called and the village lads rushed forward to claim their prize.

September 5th, Wednesday

My venture in the wheatfields has left me covered in the bites of harvest-mites, and no amount of scratching will relieve the itch.

October 10th, Wednesday

While crossing the Bailey this morn I heard a great commotion coming from beyond the castle walls. I rushed out through the gate and saw a crowd of villagers. In their midst was the Reeve, followed by David. Behind both walked the Water-Keeper. In one hand he carried a small fish, and in the other he held a rope which was tied to David's wrists.

They walked with difficulty toward the castle gate, for the angry crowd slowed their pace. I saw many that I knew from the harvest.

Mark was there, too, so I asked him what had happened.

"Our Water-Keeper is all for locking David up, just for poaching a tiddler from the castle moat," he replied scornfully. "He lay in wait all night to catch him!"

At this I swear my mouth must have gaped, for I had thought David's ventures a secret only he and I shared. This made Mark laugh. "Didst thou not know? Fie, man, everyone in the village takes fish, and hare and pheasant!

Thus folk are angry, for they guess the Water-Keeper chose David on purpose, to warn others."

October 11th, Thursday

David is locked up beneath the gatehouse tower. Though he is a guest in the castle, he is an unwelcome one and would both starve and freeze if his daughter did not bring food and firewood to his cell. By crouching low I can peer in through a grating and look down into his cell. It is small and cramped, and so dark that I can scarce make out his face. It must be damp, too, for the moat is hard by, but he complains not.

October 22nd, Monday

Still David is kept within the cell. It seems he must stay there until the castle court meets next month. Small crimes my uncle judges, and chooses the punishment. But because David's crime is serious, the King's judge must decide his fate, and he visits the castle only twice a year.

November 2nd, Friday

Now the weather is cold, and meat does not rot, the stockmen have begun the slaughtering. Pig and sheep are all slaughtered, save only those that are needed for breeding in the spring.

Isbel says: "Angels eat once a day, men twice, and animals thrice. Even a hayrick the size of the Keep would not feed all our livestock through the winter."

November 3rd, Saturday

I watched the pig-man kill a hog. First he fed her a bucket of acorns, and with his left hand stroked her back. Privily he held in his right hand a hammer. With this he did strike a blow to her head while her snout was in the bucket.

The blow felled her, and quick as a flash he cut her throat. Blood pumped into a bucket that stood ready, for nothing be wasted and blood makes a fine sausage.

I asked him how his left hand could be so kind, yet his right hand so cruel.

"Not cruel, lad," he replied. "Hogs live only for the
day when they shall die and feed us. Yet not kind, either.
We do stroke the hogs to calm them, for a happy hog
makes tastier bacon!"

The meat must all be trimmed and cut and packed in
barrels full of salt to last the winter. But not even salt will
preserve the innards for long, so even the lowest servants
can gorge themselves on brains and tripe and blood
sausage, and for once all our bellies are full.

November 5th, Monday

David will be tried soon. I asked of Simon what would happen to him. "Yonder poacher?" he replied. "Let him rot in jail for stealing our fish." But when I pressed him, he continued. "Poaching is a felony, so if the court finds him guilty, he shall be turned off."

At lessons later, I asked Mark what was meant by "turned off." He whispered back, "Why, hanged, you oaf! Executed." This so alarmed me that I dropped my tablet, cracking it into five pieces. Beaten once for each piece.

November 9th, Friday

The stockmen gave Humphrey some pigs' bladders. These we puffed up with air and sailed on the moat. At dinner we ate round, sweet puddings made of more such bladders, filled with pig fat and fruit, and then boiled.

November 22nd, Thursday

Tomorrow the Judge arrives to hear the cases that are to
be brought before the castle court. The Judge is the
King's official. It is his job to travel the countryside
hereabouts to ensure that lawbreakers are fairly tried.

The court is held in the Great Hall, and Mark has
explained to me how it will be (for he has watched
before). The Constable brings in each wrongdoer in turn,
and a jury, which is twelve men chosen from the village,
listens to the story of their crime. If the jurymen agree a
prisoner has done wrong, the Judge decides what the
punishment will be. If they think not, then the prisoner
is not guilty and is set free.

November 23rd, Friday

I crept into the Hall this forenoon to watch the court.
First the Water-Keeper recounted David's capture — he
was trapped with the fish in his hand, and two rabbits in
his bag. All were the property of my uncle. David hung

his head and my heart sank, for I feared no one would doubt his crime.

When David had spoken for himself, another from the village vouched that he was a good and godly man. But the Judge did not agree.

"Well, jurymen," saith the Judge. "You cannot doubt that this man is a poacher and a rogue. 'Tis clear he should hang this day." He let out a deep sigh, and asked: "Come men, what say you? Surely he is guilty?"

I held my breath while the jurors talked softly. Then the foreman (who is their leader) spoke: "Aye, sir, we all agree…"

The Judge turned to look at David. But then the foreman continued, "We all agree that he be not guilty as we see it."

At this the Reeve jumped to his feet and slammed his fist on the table. "Hell's teeth!" he shouted. "Shall we never stop these outrages?" The Constable scowled at David, and jerked his head to show that he could leave.

I jumped for joy to hear that David would be free, and rushed to tell Mark. He scoffed: "The Judge is an old fool, and the Reeve twice the idiot! The villagers would not send one of their own to the hanging tree, would they? Poacher he may be, but David will never suffer more than a spell in the dungeon."

December 7th, Friday

This morn my aunt told me that my father is coming! He is expected the day after the feast of Saint Stephen, and I am to return home with him to visit with my family. I cannot wait to see my mother and sisters again, though I shall sorely miss my friends here and hope they do not forget me while I am gone.

December 19th, Wednesday

Went to cut branches of holly and ivy to hang in the
Great Hall and elsewhere. Mistletoe, too, from the apple
trees that grow by the West Wall. At first Chaplain
would not let us bring mistletoe into the Chapel. "A
pagan custom," he called it. But my aunt ignored him,
saying: "Each year it is the same. Chaplain dislikes
mistletoe because it was held holy by those who
worshiped tree-gods. But their religion is older than
Christianity, so I see little harm in it."

December 25th, Christmas Day

There was dancing and jollity in the Chapel after Mass
this day, which again made Chaplain mutter about
pagans, but he would not (or could not) stop it. High and
low danced together and those who came to wish us well
this day joined in the revelry, too. Even Chaplain tapped
his foot when he forgot he should not. Then all the castle
folk gathered in the Hall—from the Constable to the

lowliest stable-lad. To each my aunt made a gift, and all
thanked her kindly. I received an inkwell with a silver lid,
and a tiny knife to cut goose quills into pens.

December 26th, Saint Stephen's Day

Dinner in the Hall today was a grand feast in honor of the
saint. To celebrate Saint Stephen they do many things here
of which we know nothing at home. Today, I learned, is a
day for rewarding the castle horses. They are given a special
feed and do no work at all, though not even Chaplain could
explain why this was. Then the other pages and I went out
to "hunt the wren," which is yet another old custom that is
followed here. But though we took crumbs of bread and
spent much time hiding in bushes, we
could not capture so much as a
feather to show for our pains.
Had a grand snow battle,
though, at which Mark and I
were clearly the victors!

December 27th, Thursday

This day my father arrived, leading a second
horse for me. I had been looking out for
him from high up in the watchtower, and
as he neared I hastened out to greet him.

My father says we shall leave for
home early on the morrow, so I spent
what was left of the day in making my
farewells to my cousins and the many other friends that I
have made here. Mark and I looked for David in the village,
but though the fire in his house was still warm, we found
him not, so Mark will tell him I am gone.

December 28th, Friday

Father woke me before dawn. We dressed and ate so quickly
I scarce had time to hug my aunt and uncle but we were
away. It is a long ride to Saltington, and my father desired to
use every moment of daylight for travel, though the moon
would light our way should we not reach home by nightfall.

When we had gone some way off, I heard the drumming of hoofs behind us. It was Simon hastening after us. "Ho, Toby!" he hailed, and when we had halted gave me a long, slim parcel wrapped in cloth.

"Remember thine archery, Cousin," he said. "No bird is safe on the wing so long as thou practice at the butts." With this he slapped me on the back so hard I near fell in a dyke. We said one last goodbye, and he was gone again. Though I did not open my gift until we reached home, I guessed what was inside it.

As Simon left us I turned to look back at Strandborough. New-fallen snow dusted the tall towers, and on the highest I could see the watchman stamp his feet and blow on his hands to keep warm. 'Tis but a twelvemonth since I first saw that sight — yet somehow I fancied I returned home far more than a year grown.

Toby's World

TOBY'S DIARY IS A STORY, but boys like Toby really did leave their families to work as pages in castles, and would have played the games his diary describes, and met people similar to those who appear in its pages. But although Toby wouldn't have known it, his uncle's castle was nearing the end of its useful life. Castles were built to withstand attack and in 1285, Europe was at peace. When wars began again, some fifty years later, new weapons and ways of fighting gradually made castles less important.

Toby's World

High and Low

As the Baron of Strandborough, Toby's uncle would have been part of the most powerful group of noblemen in his country—second only to a king or queen.

These noble lords controlled vast areas of land and the castles that went with them. In return, they pledged their loyalty to the king and promised to fight in his wars and to bring an army of knights and foot soldiers with them. They also had to pay the king part of the wealth their lands brought them, as taxes.

Knights were noblemen who were also professional warriors. Each lord gave some of his lands and manor houses to his knights to use, to support themselves and their families. In return, the knights promised to fight for that lord and for the king.

All these noblemen had total control over the lands they were given, including the peasants—villeins and freemen—who lived and worked on their estates.

Villeins had to stay on the estate on which they were

95

Who Was Who in the 13th Century

king or queen

barons, earls, dukes, bishops, and abbots

knights, noblewomen, priests, and chaplains

freemen

and villeins

born, and could be punished for leaving it. They farmed plots of land and had to give their labor and part of their crops to the nobleman who owned the land.

Freemen had more rights. They could move to another estate, and laws limited how much labor they had to do on their lord's land. Both villeins and freemen had to fight in their lord's army, though, and provide their own weapons.

Aside from the lords and their knights, the only other people of importance were high-ranking officials of the Church, such as bishops and the abbots of monasteries. These people might also be given land, but their only duty was to pray for the lord who gave it to them.

In western Europe, this way of organizing people according to their birth and the amount of land they controlled was called feudalism. However, by 1285, knights had begun to pay money to their lord instead of fighting in his army. And eventually, money payments replaced all of the feudal duties.

Younger Sons

In Toby's time, when a nobleman died, his title and lands usually passed to his oldest son. And if he was wealthy enough, his other children might receive a "living," such as a manor house with some farmland.

As the younger son of a lord, someone like Toby's father might train as a knight but not be able to afford the expensive warhorse and armor that knights used in battle.

Instead, he could join the Church or choose simply to live off his manor by farming his lands.

For noblewomen, the only choices were to marry, to seek service with a wealthier noble-woman, or to become a nun.

A Page's Life

The sons of noblemen were often sent to live as pages in the household of a more important lord — usually by the time they were seven or eight years old. Here they were taught to hunt, to handle weapons, and to play games of skill, such as chess. They also learned how to be useful to their masters, and how to behave in noble society.

At the age of fifteen or sixteen, a page became a squire. He acted as a personal servant to his master and rode into battle with him, often taking part in the fighting.

After about five years, a squire could become a knight. Any knight could award him this honor, although it was usually done by his master or by the king.

The Castle

For hundreds of years, warfare was used throughout Europe as a means of gaining power, wealth, and land. And castles played a vital part in warfare.

A castle was a secure place from which to launch an attack, and a stronghold to retreat to after a defeat.

Castles were often built in a commanding position — to control a road or a river-crossing, or the land and people around them. And they provided safe homes, where their owners could live off the produce of their estates without fear of attack.

Like most European castles, a castle such as Strandborough would have changed over time.

New buildings and other structures would have been added to it as each generation of castle builders discovered ways of strengthening and improving its defenses.

At the beginning of the

Motte

Bailey

ditch

fence

11th century, most European castles amounted to little more than a wooden tower, surrounded by a fence and perched on top of a mound of earth called a Motte. The owner, his family, and his warrior-guards lived in the tower. Below the Motte, a second fence and a ditch enclosed a Bailey—an open space which could be used to protect local people and their livestock in times of war.

Strongholds of Stone

Motte-and-Bailey castles were quick and cheap to build, but castles of stone were stronger and provided better protection against attack by fire. Gradually, stone towers called Keeps began to replace the wood and earth fortresses, and a strong stone wall called a "curtain" wall was put around the Bailey.

Keeps varied, but most had living accommodations on upper floors, with storage rooms below. A raised doorway, reached by a staircase, allowed entrance to the Keep and was easier to defend than a door at ground level.

The weakest part of a castle wall was its gate, so this had to be especially strong. Often the gateway was part of a solidly built tower called the gatehouse.

By raising the drawbridge that spanned the ditch or moat

outside the walls, the gateway could be closed off with a solid wall of wood. Behind this, a wooden grille, called a portcullis, could be lowered so that entry was difficult even when the drawbridge was down.

Next, defensive towers were added to the curtain wall. Because the towers stuck out from the wall, archers on the top could fire down on anyone at the wall's foot.

Battlements, too, were another cunning defense. These gap-toothed wall tops allowed archers to stand safely on the wall-walk behind the raised sections while firing through the gaps in between.

By 1285, European castles had seen almost four hundred years of improvement. They had become immensely strong and almost impossible to defeat. In fact, the only reliable way to capture a castle was to surround it with a hostile army and try to starve the people inside into surrendering. This was known as putting a castle under siege.

Under Attack

By surrounding the castle, the attackers could stop food and other supplies from reaching it. Unless a supporting army could drive the attackers off, hunger would eventually force

Siege Weapons

1 MANGONEL: A large catapult powered by tightly twisted ropes, like a toy slingshot with a stretched rubber band.

2 BATTERING RAM: A heavy log swung from a wooden frame. It was used to smash through the gateway of a castle or to chip away at the walls. To protect the soldiers wielding it, the ram had a wooden roof built over it.

3 PAVISES: Large wooden shields protected the attacking archers from the defenders' arrows.

4 TREBUCHET: A giant catapult with a heavy weight at one end. Troops pulled the other end to the ground to load it with rock. When it was released, the weight crashed down and hurled the rock against the castle wall.

Rocks weren't the only missiles that were thrown, though. Trebuchets catapulted beehives, rotting animal carcasses, even human heads.

5 SPRINGALD: A huge crossbow that hurled iron spears.

6 FIRE: Flaming arrows and pots filled with burning tar were fired at wooden doors and roofs.

7 SCALING LADDERS: These were used to try to climb over the walls.

8 SIEGE TOWER: A safer way to get inside was to use a wooden siege tower. A bridge could be lowered from the top of the tower to reach the battlements. Wet hides protected it from the defenders' fire, and earned it the nickname "the bear." Filling the moat with logs and rubble allowed the attackers to roll both the ram and the bear right up to the walls.

the castle to surrender. The attackers didn't just sit around and wait, though. They looked for cracks in the castle's defenses — and if there weren't any, they did their best to make some, mostly by using enormous weapons called siege engines.

The soldiers defending the castle did everything they could to hold out against the siege. Stocks of food and drink kept in the castle storerooms were carefully rationed. (Every castle had its own well inside the Bailey or the Keep, but even this could run dry, or the attackers might find a way to poison it.)

Protective wooden covers called hoardings were built over the battlements. These jutted out from the wall and gave the archers inside them a better view of the enemy. Also, holes in the hoarding floor allowed defenders to drop rocks onto anyone who tried to scale the walls.

Wooden roofs were built over tower tops, too, and covered with soaking-wet animal hides to resist fire.

But for every clever defense that could be found to strengthen a stronghold's weak points, there was always an equally clever method of attack.

Into Battle

A siege was a costly and time consuming way to wage war. If a castle was well stocked, and its defenders determined not to give up, a siege could last for months or even years. And once the attackers had used up whatever crops or livestock they could find in the surrounding countryside, they had to bring in regular supplies of food from elsewhere, or they too would starve.

A swifter way to victory was on the battlefield. But this had its problems too. Feudal knights only had to fight for their lord for a few weeks each year. And when their duty was done they could just pack up and go home.

By Toby's time, however, lords had begun to hire knights who would continue to fight for as long as they were paid.

Battles often began with the enemy armies lined up opposite one another. Then the mounted knights charged, each aiming to knock their opponents from the saddle. Once on the ground, knights were hampered by the weight of their armor and were more easily killed or captured by the foot soldiers who followed the knights into battle.

Hand Weapons

Knights fought with swords and lances, but foot soldiers used many weapons, including swords, daggers, and pole arms—long wooden poles fitted with axes, knives, or spikes.

Pikes, for example, were like long spears. With the pole end held firmly against the ground and the point facing forward, a row of soldiers with pikes made a deadly defense against charging knights.

Another favorite pole arm was the halberd. This had both a sharp spike and an axe blade, and could be used to hook or trip an enemy as well as stab and chop at him. Armed with a halberd, a foot soldier could hack at a knight's armor or at his horse, yet stay safely out of sword range.

From the 13th century on, archers too became increasingly important on the battlefield. They used both longbows and crossbows. Longbows required more skill (to shoot accurately, archers had to train from childhood), but an expert archer could fire six arrows a minute and hit a target 100 yards away. Some could fire twice this many if their aim did not have to be accurate. A massed body of archers could make arrows fall like rain on their terrified enemy.

The crossbow had a power and range similar to a longbow, but drawing the bow (pulling back the string) and loading a bolt (a small arrow) was slow. Crossbow archers could aim and fire only one arrow a minute, but they needed very little training.

Armor

Just as castles needed strong walls, so soldiers needed strong clothing to protect them from enemy weapons. In Toby's day, the commonest form of body armor was chain mail.

Armorers made mail by linking tiny wire loops to form a kind of heavy metal fabric. A hauberk or coat of mail alone might contain 30,000 rings, each joined by hand.

A full suit of armor could weigh as much as 66 pounds. It was stuffy and hot to wear, but because the weight was spread evenly around the knight's body, he could wear it all day without becoming tired.

A Suit of Armor

A knight wore many layers of protective clothing. Getting dressed was a slow business and needed the help of a squire.

Undergarments protected the skin from bruises and rubbing:
1 DOUBLET: thick linen undershirt
2 AKETON: thickly padded undercoat
3 ARMING-CAP: padded headcover
4 LEATHER SHOES

Next the chain mail:
5 COIF: mail covering for head
6 HAUBERK: coat of mail
7 MAIL HOSE

Then came a layer of metal and hardened leather:
8 A COAT OF PLATES: like a leather jerkin lined with small overlapping steel scales
9 GAMBOISED CUISSES: quilted tubes (like legwarmers), pulled over the thighs
10 SCHYNBALD: shin guards of boiled leather
11 POLEYNS: metal kneepads
12 ESPAULERS: metal shoulder plates

And the final touches:
13 SURCOAT: long linen overcoat decorated with the knight's coat of arms
14 AILETTES: decorative shoulder pieces made of parchment or thin wood
15 BELT AND SWORD in a leather scabbard
16 GAUNTLETS: mail mittens or gloves
17 HELM with crest
18 WOODEN SHIELD

A suit of armor like this was worn for tournaments. In battle, knights wore a lighter helm and less decorative armor.

The cost of a full suit of armor and a trained warhorse was very high and only the richest knights could afford them. Poorer knights often made do with bits of armor picked up from the battlefield or handed down to them from their fathers.

Foot soldiers wore far less armor than knights. They had to provide their own and few could afford to do this. Many had only a metal helmet to protect them, although a better equipped soldier might also wear a short-sleeved hauberk and a coif—a mail headcovering worn beneath the helmet.

Friend or Foe?

At the tournament or on the battlefield, colorful patterns called arms shone from shields and fluttered on flags. The use of arms began in the first half of the 12th century, as a way of helping knights to tell friend from foe on the battle-field when helmets hid their faces.

Each noble family had its own unique design, and at first these were made up of simple shapes, such as stripes or crosses. The designs soon became more elaborate, though, including real or imaginary animals (such as the ravens on Toby's uncle's arms) or objects like castles or swords.

The design was held within the shape of a shield, and when noble men and women married, they joined the shields of their families together to make a new one. Usually they did this by painting the husband's arms on one half of the shield and his wife's on the other. And when their children married, they divided the shield yet again, into quarters. So the arms of each generation became more and more complicated.

man's shield

woman's shield

joined shield

Keeping track of all these designs was the job of heralds, and eventually this work, and the knowledge of how each design was constructed and what each part of it meant, became known as heraldry. Heralds had other tasks as well, though. They organized tournaments and other ceremonies, and acted as messengers on the battlefield, carrying instructions to troops.

Changing Times

As Toby was writing his diary, knowledge of a terrible new weapon was spreading across Europe. Over the centuries that followed, cannons would transform warfare — and in particular the role of castles.

Cannons were small and limited in range at first. But as they became more powerful, they were used with increasing success for destroying castle walls.

Thicker walls gave castles added protection, but by the 15th century, cannons had become so effective that no wall could withstand their pounding.

Cannons, then, made castles useless, but other events had already begun their decline.

During the 14th century, the plague known as the Black Death killed more than a third of Europe's people. Skilled workers were in short supply, and those who had survived demanded better wages. This added to the already high cost of building a castle, so fewer and fewer new ones were constructed.

Feudalism was changing, too, and the kings and queens of Europe were helping to destroy it. They knew that a bold lord who held many lands and castles could build up a strong army around him and could challenge their power — and some did. So they discouraged castle building, and banned lords from keeping private armies. In their place marched loyal knights who obeyed only royal commands.

By the 16th century, the age of the great fortress castle had come to an end. A hundred years later, many castles were in ruins, and Toby's colorful world had vanished for ever.

Glossary and Index

Page numbers that are <u>underlined</u> show where unusual words from castle times have already been explained—other unusual words are explained here. Words shown in *italics* have their own entries, with more information or pages to look up.

A

ACRE 73 About as much land as an ox could plough in a day.

ALE 15, 32, 57, 63, 75 Alcohol brewed from barley.

ANVIL 48 An iron block on which metal is beaten into shape.

APPRENTICE 41 A trainee.

ARCHER 38, 101, 104, <u>106–107</u>

ARCHERY 35–39, 90, <u>106</u>

ARMOR 40, 45, 51, 97, <u>107–109</u>

ARMORER <u>41</u>, 107

ARMORY 4–5, <u>40</u>, 48

ARMS (HERALDIC) 45, 108, <u>109–110</u>

ARMY 95, 97, 112

ARROW 36–39, 103, 106

B

BAILEY 4–5, 9, 51, 53, <u>100</u>

BANQUET 55, 58–64

BATTERING RAM <u>102</u>

BATTLE 105, 108

BATTLEMENTS <u>101</u>, 104

"BEAR" <u>103</u>

BILE 68 A fluid from the liver. Black bile was thought to be one of the four *humors: melancholia.*

BLACK DEATH 111 A terrible *plague* in the mid 14th century. Large swellings under the skin turned black and then burst.

C

COAT OF MAIL 51, <u>107</u>, 108
COCKATRICE <u>62</u>
COCK-CROW 51, 76
Daybreak, or any other time of
day at which a rooster crows
(which is often).
COLEE <u>52</u>
COMBATANT 49 A person
taking part in a combat or fight.
CONSTABLE <u>17</u>, 35, 83
COOK 31–34, 72, 75
COURT 79, 82, 83
CROSSBOW <u>107</u>
CUP-BEARER 63 The servant
whose job it was to fill people's
drinking cups at a *banquet*.
CURTAIN WALL <u>100</u>

D

DANCING 86, 87
DIZZARD 39 A fool or jester.
DOCTOR 65–68
DOGS 25–29
DRAWBRIDGE 4–5, 100–101
DUB 51 To make a *squire* into

a *knight* in a special ceremony.
DUNGEON 85
DYKE 90 A ditch.

E

EARL 55–56, 58, 62, 96 One
of the highest ranks of *nobility*
below the king.
EGYPTIACAL COTTON 41
Cotton from Egypt, and quite
costly in Toby's day.
EGYPTY DAY <u>50</u>
ESTATE 17, 56, 95–96
Property, including a castle or
manor house and its lands.
EWE 76 A female sheep.

F

FANFARE 63 A musical blast
on a *horn* to announce an important person or event.
FARE 63 Food.
FARTHING 57 A silver coin
worth 1/4 of an old penny.
FASHION 37 To make.

FEAST 52, 58–64, 88

FEIGN 49, 69 To fake.

FELONY 82 A serious crime.

FEUDALISM 95–97, 111

FINGER PILLORY 24 (Larger, public pillories held criminals so that passers-by could hurl insults and rubbish at them.)

FIRE 103

FISH 42, 69, 70, 72, 78, 82

FISH DAY 42 One of the days on which the *Church* forbade meat, so people ate fish instead.

FLIGHT 37 The feathers at the tail end of an *arrow*.

FOOD 31–35, 58–64, 101, 104

FOOT SOLDIER 95, 106, 109

FORENOON 21 Morning.

FOWL 62 Any bird suitable for eating.

FREEMAN 96–97 Unlike a *villein*, a freeman or freewoman could choose where to live and work. Their children were born with the same rights.

FURNACE 40 A very hot fire.

G

GARB 41 Clothing.

GARDEROBE 53, 54 Originally a room for storing clothes, but also a polite term for a lavatory.

GATEHOUSE 4–5, 79, 100

GONG-FARMER 54

GREAT CHAMBER 4–5, 17, 66

GREAT HALL 4–5, 9, 10, 25, 52, 58, 83, 86

GUARD 35

H

HALBERD 106

HALL See *Great Hall*.

HARVEST 71, 72–77

HEATHEN 50 Non-Christian.

HELM 40, 45, 48, 49, 51, 108 A type of helmet, encasing the entire head.

HELMET 108, 109

HERALD 45, 48, 49, 110

HERALDRY 110

J

K

L

Romans, and still used for the *Church*, the law, and scholarship in the *Middle Ages*.

LISTS <u>44</u>

"LIVING" 97 Land and property providing a home and an income.

LONGBOW <u>106–107</u>

LONGSHANKS <u>30</u>

LORD 95 A nobleman to whom other *knights* owed allegiance.

LORD'S DAY, THE 14 Sunday: a holy day for Christians.

M

MAIL <u>107–109</u>

MANGONEL <u>102</u>

MANOR 18, 25, 97 The *estate* or lands that a castle controlled.

MASS 51, 86 The main religious service of the *Church*.

MEDIEVAL Of the Middle Ages (4th–15th century A.D.).

MELANCHOLIA 66 One of the four *humors*: feeling low.

MIDDLE AGES The period from the 4th to 15th century A.D.

MILE 8 (1 mile = 1.61 km)

MILLER <u>35</u>

MINSTREL 57, 63–64 A singer, poet, and musician.

MISER 75 Someone who is mean with money.

MISTLETOE 86

MOAT 4–5, 53–54, 100, 103 A deep trench surrounding a castle, sometimes filled with water.

MOONLING 41 Idiot: an insult based on the belief that the Moon could make you act oddly.

MORTALLY 50 Fatally.

MOTTE 99, <u>100</u>

N

NEEDLEPOINT 67 Embroidery.

NIGGET 41 Insect: an insult.

NOBLES 95 The class of people who are wealthy, powerful, and important, by birth.

P

PACE 44, 75 The distance between your footprints as you walk, about 30 inches. (2000 paces = 1 mile)

PAGAN 86 Non-Christian.

PAGE 7, 9–10, _12–13_, 98

PALFREY _22–23_, 52

PARCHMENT 31, 65 Beaten animal skin, used instead of paper for writing.

PAVISE _103_

PENNANT 44 A small, pointed flag, displaying heraldic _arms_.

PENNY ALE 63 A weak and therefore cheap _ale_.

PHYSICIAN 65–68 A doctor.

PIG-MAN 80

PIKE 106 A _pole arm_.

PILLORY See _finger pillory_.

PLAGUE 111 A deadly and highly contagious disease, such as the _Black Death_.

PLAYERS 57 Entertainers: actors, musicians, and acrobats.

POACHER 70, 72, 73, 74, 82, 84 A thief who hunts fish or game on someone else's property.

POLE ARM _106_

PORTCULLIS _101_

PREVAIL 44 To win.

PRIVILY 80 Secretly.

Q R

QUILL 42, 88 A feather used as a pen until the 19th century.

RAM See _battering ram_.

REAP 72 To harvest a crop.

REAPER 74, 75

REEVE _17–18_, 71–74, 76, 77

S

SAINT GEORGE'S DAY 40, 44 April 23rd: a holiday in memory of England's patron saint.

SAINT STEPHEN'S DAY 88 December 26th: a holiday in memory of the first Christian martyr.

SALLY PORT 30 A castle's back door, often a secret escape route.

Sources

Writers and illustrators owe a debt of gratitude to the authors and artists whose works inspire them. Richard Platt and Chris Riddell are especially grateful, because they searched in more than sixty books for details that would make the text and pictures of *Castle Diary* authentic. There isn't room here to list them all, but the following are among the more recently published books.

Bottomley, Frank: **Castle Explorer's Guide**

Bradbury, Jim: **The Mediaeval Archer**

Broughton, Bradford B.: **Dictionary of Medieval Knighthood and Chivalry**

Edge, David, & Paddock, John Miles: **Arms and Armour of the Medieval Knight**

Keen, Maurice: **English Society in the Later Middle Ages 1348–1500**

Koch, H.W.: **Medieval Warfare**

Leyser, Henrietta: **Medieval Women**

Miller, Edward, & Hatcher, John: **Medieval England: Rural Society and Economic Change, 1086–1348**

Muir, Richard: **Castles and Strongholds**

Nicole, David: **The Hamlyn History of Medieval Life**

Norman, A.V.B., & Pottinger, Don: **English Weapons and Warfare 449–1660**

Pounds, N.J.G.: **The Medieval Castle in England and Wales**

Prestwich, Michael: **Armies and Warfare in the Middle Ages**

Saul, Nigel: **The Oxford Illustrated History of Medieval England**

Warner, Philip: **The Medieval Castle (Life in a Fortress in Peace and War)**

Woodcock, Thomas, & Robinson, John Martin: **The Oxford Guide to Heraldry**

Thanks are also due to the unknown artists who decorated **The Luttrell Psalter** (for Sir Geoffrey Luttrell of Lincolnshire in about 1330) with superb scenes of medieval life.

And to the staff of **Manorbier Castle** in Dyfed, Wales.

RICHARD PLATT has written numerous nonfiction books for children, including *Pirate Diary*, also illustrated by Chris Riddell, and *Roman Diary*, illustrated by David Parkins. His favorite subjects are castles and all things medieval.

CHRIS RIDDELL'S glorious illustrations spill off the pages of many wonderful children's books, including Richard Platt's *Pirate Diary* and *Jonathan Swift's Gulliver*, abridged by Martin Jenkins.

PIRATE DIARY
THE JOURNAL OF JAKE CARPENTER, CABIN BOY

Beginning in 1716, *Pirate Diary* recounts the adventures of nine-year-old Jake Carpenter as he discovers the thrills and perils of life on the high seas.

ROMAN DIARY
THE JOURNAL OF ILIONA, SLAVE GIRL

The year is AD 107 and Iliona, an educated Greek girl, has been orphaned and sold as a slave in Rome. Apart from her beloved diary, she hasn't a friend in the world. . . .